This Ladybird book belongs to:

For my children, Albie, Elsie and Stanley.
I'll see you when Wednesday comes . . .

P. E.

For my family – both the one I grew up in
and the one I am a part of making.

J. R.

LADYBIRD BOOKS

UK | USA | Canada | Ireland | Australia
India | New Zealand | South Africa

Ladybird Books is part of the Penguin Random House group of companies
whose addresses can be found at global.penguinrandomhouse.com.

www.penguin.co.uk   www.puffin.co.uk   www.ladybird.co.uk

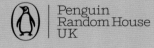

Penguin
Random House
UK

First published 2023
002

Illustrated by Jess Rose
Illustrations copyright © Ladybird Books Ltd, 2023
Text copyright © Phil Earle, 2023
Moral rights asserted

Printed in China

The authorized representative in the EEA is Penguin Random House Ireland,
Morrison Chambers, 32 Nassau Street, Dublin D02 YH68

A CIP catalogue record for this book is available from the British Library

ISBN: 978–0–241–52952–2

All correspondence to:
Ladybird Books Ltd
Penguin Random House Children's
One Embassy Gardens, 8 Viaduct Gardens
London SW11 7BW

TWO PLACES TO CALL HOME

Phil Earle   Jess Rose

Meet Florrie!

Florrie has TWO of everything.

Two *lovely* brothers . . .

two smashing
parents . . .

two very
cuddled pets.

But two wasn't *always* a magic number, as Florrie
now had to live in TWO different homes:

one with her mum . . .

and one with her dad.

When her parents separated, everything felt so different,
and Florrie was left sad and confused.

"We'll still be a family," Dad said. "We'll just be a family
that doesn't live under the same roof."

Florrie still didn't like it.
In fact, she was worried.

Her rucksack,
packed for Mum's,
felt like it had
eight elephants
crammed inside.

"I want things to be like before. I can't live
in two different places, Dad." said Florrie.
"I'm not brave enough!"

"You're so brave . . ." said Dad, "or I hope you are, as we
have to go on a special adventure before you leave for Mum's.
Meet me in the living room wearing ALL your warmest clothes."

Ten minutes later, the icy winds
nipped at Florrie's nose
on the **highest mountain**
in the whole world.

"What are we doing up here?" She shivered.

"At the top of the mountain is a special stone that grants bravery to the person who finds it," replied Dad.

Florrie clambered on.

It was cold and tiring, but when she spotted the stone and hid it safely in her pocket it was worth it!

She liked how it felt there.
It made her feel warm . . .

and braver.

"Take it to Mum's," Dad said.
"If ever you don't feel brave, rubbing
the special stone will help. I promise."

After a longer-than-normal hug,
Florrie left for Mum's, her pocket glowing as she walked.

Florrie's time with Mum
was magical.

They played and
they laughed . . .

they read and
they coloured.

And, when she missed Dad,
the special stone in her
pocket was there to help her.

But, the night before she was going to go back to Dad's, Florrie felt worried.

"What's wrong?" asked Mum.
"I can't live in two different places,"
said Florrie. "I'm not brave enough!"

"You totally are," chuckled Mum.
"Meet me in the garden with your torch,"
said Mum. "You'll see."

Ten minutes later,
they were hurtling
through space on their
way to the moon.

"What's our mission, Mum?"
Florrie asked.

"To bring home a magical moon flower,"
said Mum. "But only the bravest child
will know where to look for it."

Florrie looked high . . .

and low . . .

but never
once gave up.
She found it growing
behind a space rock.

Mum made it
into a necklace . . .

And Florrie wore
it proudly.

It made her feel braver, too – so brave she even told Mum
to turn the hall light out at bedtime.

The next day, after a longer-than-normal hug,
Florrie left for Dad's.

Florrie had the best time back at Dad's!

They cycled and
they giggled . . .

they swam and
they drew.

And, every time Florrie
remembered Mum,
she held the necklace
and knew she wasn't
far away.

That evening, Dad and Florrie baked up a storm.

"I should go to Mum's now," Florrie said,
licking the chocolate off the spoon. "Because
if I don't go then I can't come back, can I?"

"You're right!" Dad said.
"You're a genius as well as brave."

But as Florrie looked at Dad, she saw that he
didn't look brave now. He looked worried instead.

But it was OK. Florrie knew how that felt,
so she knew exactly what to do . . .

"This cake we made
is bravery cake,"
said Florrie, as she fed
Dad a HUGE slice.

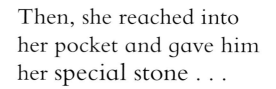

Then, she reached into
her pocket and gave him
her special stone . . .

and the magic
moon-flower necklace
because she didn't need
them any more.

Meet Florrie!
Florrie has two
of everything.

Two *lovely* brothers . . .

two smashing parents . . .

two very cuddled pets.

She even lives in
two different homes:

one with her dad . . .

and one with her mum.

And do you know what?

She absolutely loves them both.